SOMEONE OLD

SUSAN CRAWFORD

LACY WILLIAMS

I can't do this.

Claire Davidson held the notecard in trembling hands, her eyes blurring with tears and obscuring the words that were now burned into her brain. *Not right for each other. Mistake.*

They'd been planning their wedding for four months, and the morning of the big event was when it occurred to Nicholas that she was wrong for him?

She couldn't move. It was an hour to go time, and her groom had just sent a note—a note!—to call off their wedding.

"Is he in his room?" she asked Wilder, the groom's older brother, best man, and note-deliverer, who was hovering in the hall doorway and making eyes at her maid of honor, Quinn, across the room.

SUSAN CRAWFORD & LACY WILLIAMS

Quinn hadn't noticed yet that anything was wrong. She studiously ignored him as she sat in the curved alcove that housed a built-in window seat and stared out through a decades-old glass pane. And thank goodness, because Claire couldn't handle a budding romance right now. Even if it was her best friend.

The entire wedding party had been sequestered at the Sawyer Creek Bed & Breakfast for two days, preparing for her wedding to Nicholas. The mother-of-the-groom and Claire's other bridesmaid, Shelby, had gone downstairs to welcome the arriving guests. Until a few minutes ago, Claire had watched from the upstairs window as several people in their wedding finest emerged from their cars.

An ache spread through her chest, and she realized she was white-knuckling the notecard. She had to stay calm.

"Is he?" she demanded of Wilder, who was still gazing at Quinn. Claire stepped toward him, the massive amounts of tulle in her skirt whispering delicately.

It was enough to snap him out of his distraction. He shook his head. "What? No. He's gone."

Her groom. Gone.

No.

No, no, no.

This couldn't be happening.

"Gone? Who, Nicholas? Where?" Quinn's voice was full of force as she stood from the window seat.

"I don't know." Wilder's misery was plain to see in the tight way he held himself, the frown he wore. Something had definitely been going on between him and Quinn this weekend. Claire had been sure of it. But now her best friend was avoiding Wilder's eyes, and she'd been quiet all morning.

Claire didn't have time to wonder about her best friend's love life. Especially since her own was currently crashing to a halt. "Is he still on the property?"

The B&B had a lovely lawn—which had been spread with white wooden chairs—and a sprawling garden, a gazebo, and even a thicket of pine trees at the far end where the property hadn't been developed yet. If Nicholas was still around somewhere, she could talk to him. Make him explain himself.

Was this just a case of cold feet? It had to be, right? It was like something from a bad romance novel. In real life, a groom didn't run out on his bride right before it was time to walk down the aisle.

"I don't know if he's still around," Wilder said, breaking her from the train wreck of her thoughts.

"I'll find him." Quinn stood with a rustle of satin. The wine-colored floor-length gown she wore made her seem even taller than her five feet ten inches. She pulled a pair of flip flops from the open suitcase and slipped them on—an image that was so very *Quinn*. "Maybe Shelby knows something." Nicholas's younger sister was a long shot, though. She'd been away from Sawyer Creek a long time. Claire had asked her to be a bridesmaid mostly out of courtesy. She'd been shocked when she agreed.

"I'll go, too," Wilder said.

Quinn hadn't looked at him once since he'd appeared in the doorway, tense and unhappy. Now her gaze snapped to him.

He winced under its intensity.

"I think you've done enough," Quinn mumbled as she headed for the door.

"Quinn—"

Whatever Wilder said to her was lost as the door closed behind them. Claire *knew* something had happened between them, but her friend's broken heart was a worry for later.

Mistake. Not right for each other.

How could Nicholas write those things?

Her knees wobbled, and the emotion she'd been trying to hold at bay hit her like a tidal wave.

4

She took one step and leaned her shoulder against the wall. With the layers of her petticoat and the massive tulle skirt of the wedding dress itself, there was no way she could sit.

Standing here gave her a perfect view out the large window, framed with gauzy white curtains. More cars were arriving, spilling onto the overflow parking area and blocking in the cars parked nearer the B&B, which was really an older farmhouse that had been lovingly restored.

Was Nicholas's car still here? Was he?

Her eyes strained to see.

Not right for each other.

They *were* right for each other. She'd spent the last two and a half years of her life proving it.

From the moment he'd asked her out in a coffee shop after her Complex Nursing Care class, Claire had done everything in her power to be what he wanted. Because she loved him, and she refused to lose this one.

When he'd deferred to her, she'd chosen restaurants for their dates that he'd mentioned he liked. She'd worn feminine dresses he appreciated. Because he was a physician, she'd read more medical books than her nursing degree required, so she'd be able to converse intelligently about family medicine. She'd even let her dad back into her life after years of separation. All because Nicholas had encouraged her to.

And her dad was supposed to walk her down the aisle in—she glanced at the time—half an hour.

Claire glanced away from the pearl face of her gold wristwatch, a gift from her late grandmother when she'd been a teenager. How had so many minutes slipped away already?

Where was Nicholas?

A black truck turned down the B&B's driveway and parked at the far end of a haphazard row of cars. It looked brand new, not even a hint of the layer of dust that the cars and trucks in this small farm town tended to carry.

The man who emerged was not Nicholas. Nicholas had dark hair while this man was blond.

But Not-Nicholas seemed familiar to her, even from this distance. His body was mostly blocked by the bed of his truck. All Claire could see were his head and a pair of broad shoulders. Was he wearing a T-shirt? She couldn't tell for sure, but it sure didn't seem he was dressed for a wedding.

And then, his head turned, and he seemed to stare straight at her.

Her breath caught.

Oh, she'd seen him before all right. For a time

back in college, and then again on every third bill-board along the highway as she'd driven here from Austin. Someone in the MLB's marketing depart-ment had come up with a brilliant idea to plaster his image—his sexy, smiling face beneath a Dallas Coyotes ball cap—with the slogan *Prodigal Pitcher Returns*.

Claire hated baseball.

And she hated Jax Morris even more.

What was he doing here? He wasn't approaching the B&B. He held a cell phone to one ear. He stood casually, one hand on the bed of his pickup truck. While her life imploded.

He had some nerve showing up at her wedding. When they'd dated—could the brief fling they'd had even be called dating?—he'd never come to Sawyer Creek with her. But now that he was a local celebrity, the town gossips would have a field day.

Then a terrible thought occurred to her. Was he crashing the wedding to break it up?

It seemed preposterous, given that she hadn't seen him in three years.

Except... she was missing a groom.

Was it possible the two were related?

Had Jax done this? Had he somehow pushed Nicholas to run out on her?

She'd kill him.

She didn't think as she crossed the room and stormed down the back staircase of the B&B. She emerged at the side of the big farmhouse and pushed out onto the wrap-around porch, the humid summer air blasting her skin and draping her like a sticky blanket.

She rounded the house, grabbing handfuls of her skirt to hold it above the ground as she stomped through the gravel parking lot toward the man who'd been the first—no, second—to run out on her.

With each step closer to his massive black truck, her head of steam grew.

I can't do this.

The words Nicholas had written were an echo of what Jax had said to her so long ago. The hurt from it had dissipated by now, but anger remained. And the anger propelled her toward him.

Someone called out to her from the other side of the parking area, but she ignored the arriving wedding guest.

Jax rounded the truck as she approached and stood there with his hands in his jeans' pockets, a crooked smile on his gorgeous face. One that had made her stomach swoop in a former life.

Not now.

"Claire. You look good."

She slapped him across the face. Hard.

JAX SHOULDN'T HAVE COME.

Claire's slap had been hard enough to snap his head to one side. His cheek stung and his ears rang.

He'd known this was a mistake, but then he'd never been the smartest kid on the playground. Or the ball field, as it were.

He exhaled the air that her blow had caught in his chest.

He'd probably deserved that. For leaving like he had, and for so much more.

"Where is he?" she demanded.

Her hazel eyes were bright and her color was high, her cheeks flushed behind the striking makeup. Her blond hair was in some kind of twist, and that dress... It was a heart attack waiting to happen to the guy at the end of the aisle.

Who was, regrettably, not Jax. "Where's who?"

Her right hand fisted at her side, and Jax rocked back on his heels. She wouldn't catch him unaware again. He couldn't show up for photo day with a black eye. The P.R. people would hate him. And he figured he was only getting one shot at the majors.

"Nicholas." She hissed the word. "Where is he? What'd you say to him?"

Her rapid-fire questions made no sense whatsoever. Jax dug his hands out of his pockets to hold them up in surrender.

He instantly regretted that move. He'd stuffed his hands in his pockets to keep from reaching for her like his inner caveman wanted to do.

Mine.

Not his. Not anymore. "Who is Nicholas?"

A split-second was all it took for her to lose the fiery anger that had been directed toward him. Her face crumpled, and she pressed the fingers of one hand against the bridge of her nose. Was she crying?

"Whoa. Hey—" Like metal to a magnet, his hand stretched toward her. As soon as his fingers connected with the bare skin of her upper arm, she shook him off.

"Don't touch me!"

Right. Hands off.

She half-turned away from him, staring across the parking lot. Like she wanted to look anywhere but at him. "What are you doing here?"

That was the million-dollar question, wasn't it?

He tried to marshal his thoughts, but seeing her again had been like taking a fastball to the helmet.

He felt a little concussed. Nauseous and dizzy and short of breath.

She was getting married. Now. All dolled up and dressed up, and he'd lost his chance when he'd walked away.

"I got called up to the Coyotes." He wanted to kick himself for the inane statement.

She seemed to want to kick him, too, if the flash of anger in her eyes and still-fisted hands were any indication. "So you...came home to Texas and decided to look me up?"

Came home.

Nope. *Home* wasn't even in his vocabulary. He may have returned to the state he'd grown up in, but he'd never go back to the double-wide black hole in the wretched little town he'd scratched and clawed his way out of.

"You might've picked a better day for your blast to the past," she said. "Or whatever this is."

Yeah. No kidding. He should go.

But Claire was near tears, her gaze scanning everywhere.

He'd upset her. On her wedding day.

And something inside him wouldn't let him walk away.

He was surprised he still had the power to hurt

11

her, at least to the point of tears. The Claire he'd known had been fiercely independent and guarded with her emotions. He'd fallen in love quickly, but he'd had his own reasons for keeping his feelings to himself. It'd taken her almost a month to confess how she felt—the fact that she'd loved him at all still shocked him all these years later.

He'd come this far hoping some kernel of what she'd once felt was still alive. And maybe it was, if she was crying over him.

But suddenly, it hit him that she hadn't been paying attention to him at all, even while she'd been talking to him. She was looking for someone.

"Who's Nick?" he asked again.

"Nicholas," she repeated softly, her neck craning now.

Looking for her groom?

"Claire!" A man's voice rang out, and Claire whirled to find the source. An older man was frantically weaving his way through the parked vehicles toward them.

She picked up her skirt and started that direction.

Jax followed her. He had to. Because, like a perfect pitch, she'd just flown through his strike zone, and he couldn't *not* take a swing.

"Dad, what—?"

Dad. She'd been estranged from her father when Jax had known her. Unless this was the groom's dad. But no, the man's eyes were the same color as Claire's. And the shape of his jaw... this had to be her father.

"I just ran into Quinn in the foyer," the man said. "She said Nicholas is missing?"

Ah, good old Quinn. Claire's best friend had never liked Jax. Smart girl.

The older man shot a suspicious glance over Claire's shoulder to him. Jax had been on the receiving end of that look too many times, but within seconds, both recognition and surprise flared in the man's eyes. They'd never met before, so he must've been a baseball fan.

"He's not missing. Not exactly." Claire shot a glance over her shoulder, too, but it was full of fury. And a little secrecy.

"Then, where is my future son-in-law?" Her dad was breathing heavily, and he leaned one hand on the side of an SUV for balance.

Jax experienced a moment of elation. He'd been right. She was looking for the groom. Who had... abandoned her?

Hope fluttered, reviving his battered heart. If she

wasn't getting married today, maybe there was still a chance for him. For them.

"Claire..." He'd barely gotten her name out when all the color leached from her father's face. The man staggered and collapsed.

"Dad!" Claire cried.

Jax jumped forward, but she beat him there. Kneeling on the ground near her dad's head, it seemed she'd totally forgotten about her wedding dress. Miles of fabric were in the way as she tried to shift him from his face-down position.

"Let me help," Jax said.

She hesitated, her hands poised as though she might slap him away.

"You want me to roll him over?"

She nodded.

Jax gently turned the man to his back.

With steady movements, Claire pressed her fingers to her dad's neck to check his pulse and bent close to listen to his breathing. Her demeanor was controlled. Clinical. Had she finished her nursing degree? Gone on to work as a nurse? The questions stalled in his throat. Now wasn't the time.

"His pulse is weak," she said. "He needs a doctor. Can you call 911?"

"Is there someone inside...?"

She shook her head quickly. "No one on the guest list."

Her father moaned and then seemed to rouse. His eyes blinked open slowly. "What—?"

Claire's hand on his shoulder kept him down. "You fainted, Dad. We need to get you to the hospital to get checked out."

"I'm fine." The fact that the man's mumble was barely audible and his eyes were sliding closed again seemed to bely his statement. "Just got...dizzy...for a minute."

"You didn't *just get dizzy*," she said. "You collapsed."

"Just take me inside."

Claire's lips set in a tight line, one that Jax remembered as a sign of her stubbornness. Some of the color—not all—had come back to her dad's face, and he continued to insist he was fine. Jax understood Claire's concern, but the man did seem to be recovering quickly. A trip to the E.R. was probably unnecessary.

"We're going to the hospital." Her tone left no room for negotiation. "It'll be faster to drive than wait on an ambulance."

Still pretty as a paint and stubborn as a mule.

Jax blurted out, "I'll drive."

THE ONLY REASON Claire agreed to get into Jax's truck was proximity.

He'd parked at the very edge of the parking area, while many of the other cars—including hers—were blocked in.

It would take far too long for an ambulance—and the volunteer crew—to reach the rural B&B. She would've ignored Jax completely except for the fact that her dad was leaning heavily on him to get to the truck.

Dad was still ashen. She didn't like the rattle in his breathing, but she wouldn't know for certain what was wrong until a doctor got ahold of him.

Jax boosted her dad into the passenger seat, and then shut the door. She'd planned to have Dad scoot to the middle so she wouldn't have to sit next to the man who'd abandoned her three years ago, but that didn't make sense, did it? The less Dad was moved and bumped around, the better.

She gritted her teeth as she picked up her skirt and followed Jax around the front of the truck.

He held the door open for her.

She hated the way that simple action made her *remember*.

At least he didn't try to help her in.

But her shoe caught in the mass of tulle, and she

nearly tumbled face-first into the seat. The fabric held her heel tight. She heard a distinct *rip*.

She bit her lip, blinking against hot moisture that burned her eyes. It was just a dress. She'd probably already ruined it when she'd knelt beside Dad on the muddy ground.

Jax scooped her into his arms in a perfect imitation of a *carry me over the threshold* hold. Except he wasn't her groom.

And she didn't want him holding her.

Before she could protest, he'd hefted her onto the bench seat and let her go.

All without a grunt or any sign that lifting her had fazed him at all.

Stupid man. Stupid gym rat.

He slid in beside her before she was ready, his shoulder nudging hers as she wrangled the dress beneath the steering wheel and across the seat.

She didn't want to jostle Dad, which meant she was the one jostled as Jax shut his truck door and then cranked the engine.

It was impossible to believe she could feel the press of his thigh with all the layers of tulle between them, but heat flushed up her neck and into her face anyway.

He glanced at her sideways, smiling grimly as he

put the truck in gear and eased on the gas. He'd always seen what she'd hidden so cleverly from everyone else.

She tried to shift away from him, but there was nowhere to go. So she focused intently on Dad, whose color was still bad, breathing still too shallow.

Where the gravel drive met the state highway, Jax asked, "Where's the closest hospital?"

She jerked one thumb to the right toward Sawyer Creek. "About five miles. It's the second building on Main Street. Hard to miss."

He'd probably seen it if he'd driven through the sleepy, two-stoplight town on his way to the B&B.

Way back when, he'd mentioned a couple of times that he'd like to see where she'd grown up, but she hadn't been in any rush to take him home to Sawyer Creek, figuring they had plenty of time in the future to do that. If only she'd known that *future* with Jax Morris was never meant to be.

She'd been so wrong about their trajectory. It still hurt to think about, which was why she did her best to keep a tight lid on her anguish, to keep it locked in the deepest corner of her heart.

She reached for Dad's wrist, used two fingers to take his pulse again. Still thready.

"You want to tell me why Jax Morris crashed

your wedding?" her dad asked. Even though his voice was weak, his brain seemed to be working fine.

"No idea," she said curtly.

Not that it'd stop him from prying. She'd let him back into her life a year ago to make Nicholas happy, and ever since, her relationship with her dad had been rocky at best.

He peeked around her to Jax. "Why don't you tell me then, young fellow."

Claire tried to ignore the intense silence coming off the man beside her, but she felt his gaze on her briefly before his eyes went back to the road.

Jax said nothing, which didn't keep Dad from asking more. "What's the Rookie of the Year doing with my girl?"

She wasn't his girl. Hadn't been for a long time.

Jax barked a short burst of laughter. "I'm not Rookie of the Year." *Not yet.*

Claire easily heard what he hadn't said, because she'd known him. The confidence that had come close to outright arrogance had been attractive to her once.

"With that arm and your batting average, you'll be top three by the end of this season. I've been following your career in the minors, kid."

Another glance in her direction from Dad, this one loaded.

She bared her teeth in a semblance of a smile. "Don't look at me. I hate baseball."

She'd avoided any connection to the game after Jax's desertion. It'd been a matter of self-preservation at first, then just a habit. She didn't watch games, didn't look at scores or stats. Didn't care one iota about the sport. Not even rec league stuff.

Dad groaned and shifted.

"You okay?" she asked.

"I'm not dead yet," he grouched. Maybe he didn't like her hovering. Well, too bad. There were a lot of things she didn't like about him.

He pressed on with his inquisition. "So what're you doing here, Rookie?"

Another glance from Jax. She jutted her chin out, refusing to return it. She wanted to know, too. Let him say it.

"Claire and I used to know each other."

Such a simple statement was laughable. She could only find a bitter smile. "No, we didn't."

CHAPTER 2

*O*utside the Sawyer Creek ER—if you could call a couple of curtained-off cubicles an ER—Jax sat in the tiniest waiting room he'd ever seen.

His phone buzzed in his pocket, and he tugged it free to check the display. A text message from his dad's number. Again.

Jax tapped the ignore button with reflex-like speed and shoved the phone back into his pocket. Eventually the old man would take the hint and leave him alone.

He glanced at the clock on the wall behind the registration desk. He'd been here for a half hour. After dropping Claire and her dad at the door, Jax had swung his truck around to a parking spot and jogged inside. But by the time he'd made it in, Claire was already disappearing behind one of the curtains alongside her dad.

Should he stay or go?

Claire had been less than happy to see him. And she was dealing with her dad's health issues. Not to mention her missing groom. Where the heck was the guy?

Jax couldn't wrap his mind around how somebody could be such an idiot as to be engaged to Claire—be almost to the altar!—and give her up.

Except, he'd been that much of an idiot, hadn't he?

What he was doing? He'd come to Sawyer Creek on an impulse. He'd only been called up to the Coyotes a few days ago, had been flown in to meet the owner on the team's private jet, and was officially due to report in at the practice facility in Dallas on Monday morning.

What had he expected, for Claire to have hit the pause button on her life? To have waited for him after he'd walked away? Who was he kidding?

He'd wanted to play in the majors for as long as he could remember. And after only a few weeks of playing in the minors, he was so close he could taste it. The dream had kept him alive through some very dark days.

So what did it say about him that the only thing he could think about when he'd been flying to Dallas was Claire?

He sat in the waiting room, occupied with his thoughts for who knew how long. Folks had been traipsing in and out of there, some stealing glances and some flat-out watching him, but all of them whispered. It made him uncomfortable. Is this what life in the majors would be like?

Hours later, he perked up at movement from the curtained hallway.

Claire emerged, now in a set of pale blue scrubs. She had a cell phone pressed to her ear and was speaking softly.

And Jax was enough of a jerk to strain his ears to pick up her conversation.

"—call me back. I don't know what happened. Did I say something? Do something? I—I think we could still fix things. Please. Call me back."

She wasn't speaking softly after all. Her voice was small. Broken.

Hearing it was knife to his gut.

She must've been calling the runaway groom. Jax hated that guy.

He stood and went to her.

She stared down at the phone, her nose wrinkled in consternation. She turned her head slightly at his approach, then did a double-take. "What're you doing here?"

Still not happy to see him.

"Waiting for you."

Her expression changed to wild incredulity before she blanked it. "Well, you should go home. All the way to Dallas." *Because I don't need you here.*

She returned to staring at the phone. Tapped her fingers on the screen, but she wasn't activating an app or accomplishing any task. He could see her brain working in the rapid movements of her eyes.

"How's your dad?"

"He has cancer," she snapped. "How do you think?"

Oh, Claire. He wanted to take her in his arms. Comfort her.

At the shift of his feet, her eyes darted up from the dark face of the smartphone.

Right. No touching.

He cleared his throat. "Did you know? Before today?"

Her scathing glare hit its mark, and heat ran through his chest. "Yes. We pushed up the wedding so Dad could—"

She shook her head, cutting herself off.

Acid churned in his veins. Some part of him—a glutton for punishment—asked, "Where is Nick, anyway?" The jerk should be here.

"Nicholas," she snapped again. "And it's none of your business."

Because she didn't know.

She went back to staring at the black phone screen, and he noticed her hands trembling.

"Hey." He touched her then. Couldn't keep from it. He cupped one bare elbow in his hand. "What can I do? I want to help."

She shook him off. Sniffed deeply. Wiped her cheek with one hand, even though he didn't see any sign of tears. She shook the phone angrily. "I can't… Dad is really worried about his dog being alone all night."

Hungry dog. Jax could work with that. "Do you want me to go and feed him?"

She looked at him as if he were crazy. "Do I want *you* to go and snoop through my dad's house? No thanks." Her expression changed to suspicion now.

"How long...? Why've you been sitting out here all day anyway?"

For you. Because he might be an idiot, but if there was any chance she might need him—for anything—he'd wanted to be close.

A woman in scrubs came out of a nearby door marked *Employees Only* carrying a large black garbage bag with hints of white tulle peeking through the cinched-up opening. She approached Claire, who sighed and took the bag from her hands. "Thanks." Claire held the phone out to the woman. "And thanks for letting me borrow this."

The nurse sent Jax a curious glance. "No problem, hun. Did you get ahold of who you needed to?"

Claire nodded, a wan smile on her face. But she hadn't, had she? Suddenly, her frustration over the phone made sense. She'd borrowed the phone because she must've left hers at the B&B.

"The doctor's going to keep your dad overnight, and they're both saying you should go home and rest."

Claire's lips firmed into that stubborn line, but she nodded, crossing her arms over her middle.

"I'll make sure she gets home," he said.

Claire glared at him, but the woman was already turning away, ducking back through that door.

"I don't need your help," she muttered. She stalked past the waiting room, lugging her bagged-up wedding dress toward the double sliding doors that led to the ER parking lot.

It wasn't hard for Jax to keep pace with her. "You got money on you for a cab, then?"

"No cabs in Sawyer Creek," she returned sharply.

So what was she going to do? Wave down someone she knew and ask for a ride? That didn't seem out of the realm of possibility...

But she stopped on the sidewalk outside. He stopped beside her.

Muggy air enveloped him, sticking to his skin after the A/C inside. The sun had gone down, but it hadn't helped much with the temperature.

Jax dug in his pocket, came up with his phone, and held it out to Claire.

She looked from it to his face. Her expression was carefully blank again, all hints of emotion erased.

"Somebody else you need to call?" He could out-stubborn her any day. He'd always had the skill, and they both knew it.

Finally, she shook her head slightly. "Quinn just changed her phone number. I have it programmed into my phone, but I can't remember it."

A pair of headlights swept over them as a sedan pulled into the ER parking lot.

Jax shrugged. "Then call the B&B. She's probably still there."

Claire put a hand over her face. When she spoke, her words were muffled. "I can't. Don't want to make any more of a scene. Every busybody in town is probably already talking about how I got jilted at the altar—you—this. I don't want to make things worse for Nicholas." She lifted the puffy trash bag, agitated.

Two people got out of the nearby car. One was limping badly, leaning on the other, but they both still managed to steal a glimpse of Jax and Claire.

She was right. Jax had grown up in a farm town, so he knew about local busybodies. He'd like to think the folks of Sawyer Creek would leave a dejected bride alone, but a juicy story like that would just prime the gossip pump. "I'll drive you to your dad's place."

She started to shake her head again, but as she noticed the man and woman approaching from the parking lot, she changed her mind. "Fine."

IT WAS a mistake to get into Jax's truck *again*. What if

Nicholas found out? Claire knew it, but she did it anyway. Her choices right now were severely limited.

She'd left her phone, her clothes, and her car at the B&B. Unless Quinn had moved her car, which had been the original plan.

She was supposed to have been on her honeymoon right now.

She rattled off instructions to her dad's bungalow on the other side of town. It would take five minutes to get there. Five minutes, and she'd be rid of Jax.

She couldn't believe he'd waited six hours in the ER waiting room. Did he really not have anything better to do? Or was this some desperate ploy to win her back?

She closed her eyes and leaned her head against the headrest. Dad. She needed to focus on Dad. Who'd kept insisting that things weren't as bad as they seemed. He wasn't on his deathbed yet.

His cancer diagnosis three months ago had been a nasty shock. They'd still been tiptoeing around each other after she'd made the first attempts to reconcile with him.

And then she'd felt a monumental urgency to have him be a part of her wedding. Her mom had

SUSAN CRAWFORD & LACY WILLIAMS

died years ago, and Dad was the only one left who could give her away.

And although Dad was getting around easily on his own—for now—who knew how long that would last? The doctors had only given him a fifty-percent chance of beating the cancer because of the late stage.

She'd wanted him to be a part of her wedding *now*, because he might not be here in the future.

Why had Nicholas abandoned her? He knew this was important to her. He's the one who'd pushed the reconciliation. And he'd understood her need to have her father a part of the wedding, even though it meant moving the date up. And then, he'd jilted her.

Tears stung her throat.

"This it?" Jax's gruff question had her blinking her eyes open, swallowing back the ball of grief that choked her.

He'd pulled right up to the curb. Her father's house wasn't much. Two-bedrooms, a tiny lawn that really needed to be mowed, one big picture window in the living room. Her car was nowhere to be seen. Neither was Dad's.

She hadn't thought this through. She'd been planning to use his car to drive out to the B&B later, but of course his car would be parked there.

She was so out of sorts, she couldn't think.

Jax didn't need to know any of that. His truck idling, he watched her. She could feel his gaze like a physical touch, even though she was looking out the window, pretending to ignore him.

He'd always been larger-than-life. He'd had *presence*, even as a lanky twenty-year-old.

"Thanks for the ride." She pushed open the door and slid out, wrangling her pitiful dress-in-a-bag out with her, then shut the door decisively behind her.

She prayed for him to drive away as she trudged up the sidewalk that was cracked and splintered, grass and weeds peeking through. She didn't look back.

Instead, the engine shut off. A car door opened and closed behind her.

She made it to the postage-stamp-sized front porch. *Hurry.* Where would her father hide his spare key?

There was only one flowerpot on the corner of the porch, its inhabitant long-dead. Only a scraggly brown stick poking from the dirt inside showed that anything had ever bloomed there. She tipped up the pot. No key.

Jax joined her.

She hated that she didn't have to look to know it.

Hated that his nearness could still make her heart beat faster, her skin prickle.

He didn't say anything.

Where was that key?

There were two large, flat rocks in the empty flowerbed next to the porch. She stepped off and reached for the first one. She dug her fingers into the cool soil and lifted the rock. Nothing.

"Go back home," she told Jax. "I don't want you here."

"You don't?"

She heard the arrogance in his question and turned her head to snap at him, only to find him dangling a silver key from his fingers, which were lifted above his head where he'd obviously just pulled it from the top of the outside window sill.

"I don't have a home," he said.

His words hit her squarely in the solar plexus, making her feel as if she couldn't breathe.

But whatever seriousness she'd imagined in his statement disappeared when he grinned. "I mean, they put me up in this fancy hotel for now. I'll need to shop for a new house. Something big."

For all the parties he'd no doubt throw for his teammates and whatever women he wanted around.

He hadn't meant his *I don't have a home* the way she'd taken it. He wasn't that deep. She needed to remember that. Remember exactly how shallow he'd been once upon a time, when she'd thought they were...something.

"You could come down and help me house-hunt."

"No." She stood, brushing her hand against the scrubs. She stepped back onto the porch and held her palm out.

He didn't immediately hand it to her. She saw the impulse cross his face, the hint of orneriness. He was thinking about playing keep away.

A dog barked in the background, the noise growing louder and louder from the backyard.

Finally Jax pressed the key into her palm, his fingers hot against her skin. "You sure you don't want some help? He sounds big." He tipped his head to one side, toward the sound of the yelping, which had now grown desperate.

"I'm sure." She didn't need help. Not from Jax. Not even if that dog were the size of a grizzly.

She unlocked the door, dragged her dress along, and slipped inside, shutting Jax out.

She probably should have thanked him, but she didn't feel thankful.

She felt broken. Nicholas had broken her heart, and having Jax around was shredding whatever shards were still intact.

JAX SHOULD JUST DRIVE BACK to Dallas. Obviously, Claire would be happy if he disappeared.

But he'd seen her fragility beneath the sharp exterior.

And that fragility was the reason he drove to the little diner they'd passed on the short drive from the hospital.

"We're closing up!" called a voice from the long rectangular window behind the counter.

He glanced at his wristwatch and then around the empty restaurant. Seriously? It was still early. Diners in the city would be open for another two hours, or even all night.

A door swung open, and a woman emerged from the kitchen. She wore jeans and a T-shirt with the logo of the diner across the front.

She looked surprised to see him still standing there. She jangled a huge set of keys in one hand. "Closing."

He put on his most charming smile. "I need a

favor. I'm willing to make it worth your while." He dug in his hip pocket for his wallet.

She didn't look impressed. Only suspicious.

"My friend's had a rough day. Let's just say the trip to the hospital with her father was the icing on a very bad cake. I was wondering if you could whip her up something real quick."

Her eyes went wide. "You mean Claire? You must be the guy who broke up her wedding. That baseball player."

What? Had the news really made it through town already? Small-town dynamics were nothing to mess with. Maybe this hadn't been such a brilliant idea after all. "I didn't break up her wedding. Her dad's in the hospital." He kept silent about the missing groom.

He pulled out a hundred dollar bill and plunked it on the counter. "Can you help me out?"

She stared at him for so long he started to get uncomfortable. This had been a bad idea.

But then she swept past him, scooping up the Benjamin on her way back into the kitchen. "Give me ten minutes," she threw over her shoulder.

He was left standing in the empty diner, too silent. Nothing to distract him.

I don't have a home.

What had possessed him to say that?

He'd played it off with something about how much cash he'd spend on a new house in Dallas. But the initial words had been true.

The place he'd grown up in would never qualify as a home, and he'd stopped calling it that even as a kid. He'd left at sixteen and hadn't looked back. Which made it ironic that his dad had been calling or texting at least four times a day since the news had broken about his major league deal.

During his two years at junior college, he'd lived in the cheapest off-campus apartment he could find. He'd never had company over to see the sparse, picked-up-off-the-roadside furnishings. That hadn't been home, either.

And when he'd gotten his minor league deal, he'd had his shiny new agent help him find an apartment in New Jersey. He hadn't been raking in the dough, but it'd been the nicest place he'd ever lived.

He'd been happy chasing his dreams of the bigs, or so he'd told himself. Until the words had popped out—*I don't have a home*—he hadn't realized that something was still missing for him.

Or maybe he was just tired and getting fanciful.

When the waitress brought a white to-go bag, he thanked her and got out of there. Somehow he knew that Claire wouldn't appreciate it if word got out that he was delivering food to her.

He drove back to her dad's house, but she didn't answer the door.

He tried the knob. Unlocked. Seriously. Small towns...

The house wasn't that big. He peeked in the rooms, but they were empty. No sign of life. He strode through the kitchen, leaving the bag on the table, and out the back door, where he found her sitting on the back step, one arm around a Labrador-sized dog.

The dog sensed him first, jumping up and approaching with a wildly wagging tail. He nosed Jax's thigh.

Claire stood, whirling to face him. "What're you doing—? You can't just walk in—out here."

"The front door was unlocked."

She frowned fiercely.

That's when he noticed she'd been crying. She caught his stare and attempted to wipe her cheeks, but it was too late.

That electric pull urged him to reach for her.

He didn't.

"I brought some food from the diner. In the truck, your stomach was growling so loud it was overpowering the radio."

She pressed her hands to her face, shook her head. "I can't get rid of you."

She could. He'd go if she asked him again.

But she put her hands on her hips, her chin jutting out defiantly. "Why did you come here? I want the truth."

This might be his one chance to get her to listen. He wasn't even sure what had prompted him to come, to seek her out. His head was still buzzing with the *I don't have a home*. He didn't know how to explain the mishmash of emotions crashing through him.

Her eyes never left his face.

So he told her. "I thought getting into the majors would fix what was broken inside me. And it's amazing, but... there's still something missing. I think it's because I still have feelings for you."

Her eyes went wide. She didn't say a word, just stared at him.

And then she shook her head. Shook herself out of whatever place she'd been stuck in. "I don't—I don't want your *feelings*."

The breath rushed out of him in one long exhale. He'd expected a rejection, more so after discovering exactly what he'd interrupted earlier. It still hurt.

But he stuffed his emotions away, because it was obvious she was still overwhelmed by her own.

"I want Nicholas," she said. "I need to find him. Talk to him."

Both of them were surprised when Jax said, "Okay. I'll help you find him."

CHAPTER 3

*C*laire pressed the giant, plastic-covered poof of tulle down beside her on the bench seat of Jax's truck.

As they pulled up to the B&B, there was still light shining from a few of the windows. Unlike earlier, only a handful of cars remained in the parking area, including Dad's and her own.

Thankfully, that meant there were only a few people left for Claire to steer clear of.

She didn't need the entire population of Sawyer Creek whispering about how she'd dragged her sad bag of crushed wedding dreams back into the inn. Nicholas had moved his practice here. The last thing he needed was the town gossiping about his non-wedding. Or Claire being seen with another man.

She didn't see Nicholas's SUV in the parking lot, but if she was going to find him, she needed her phone. And maybe she'd find Shelby inside.

It felt strange, to say the least, to be on the hunt for her missing groom with her ex-college fling.

Missing groom. The thought sucker-punched her as Nicholas's written words continued to assault her.

We never should've let things get this far.

What did that even mean?

Her belly was full—Jax had taken care of that with a turkey melt and french fries from the diner—and now he was delivering her back to the scene of the crime, as it were.

She tried to ignore the man, who'd followed her out of his truck and up the stairs to the huge wrap-around porch. She headed for the side door first to see if it was unlocked, hoping she could sneak in and avoid being seen by anyone who'd stayed to gawk.

"So, how'd you and good 'ol Nick meet?" Jax had been mostly-silent while they'd downed the food standing in her dad's kitchen and then on the way here.

I think I still have feelings for you. Claire was still reeling from his revelation. How could he walk back into her life and declare such a thing just a few hours later? They hadn't seen each other in three years.

"*Nicholas* and I met just after my junior year. Quinn set us up, actually."

"Good 'ol Quinn." Sarcasm laced his words.

He'd said something similar earlier, but it had sailed past her in the blur of caring for her father. She'd forgotten how he and Quinn had butted heads when she and Jax had dated.

"Quinn stuck," she said. *You didn't.*

Claire tried not to think about the dark place she'd spiraled to after Jax had left. She'd had no desire to go to class. Couldn't focus. Studying became difficult when, prior to that, it'd been as easy as breathing.

Quinn had gotten her through it, mostly by pushing Claire to get out of bed on days when she wanted to stay in her cocoon and rot.

She was never going back there. She and Nicholas had a healthy relationship. They knew each other's preferences and life goals. They knew the number of kids they wanted when they were ready to start a family in a few years. There were no secrets, no surprises—at least there hadn't been until she'd received his note earlier today.

Even so, she didn't feel the shadows lurking, waiting to overtake her if she didn't find him. Not like the pit of desperation that had opened up and swallowed her alive when Jax had left.

It was because she still had hope. Her hope was keeping that darkness away.

She loved Nicholas just as much—more!—than she'd ever loved Jax. Not that it was a competition. Nicholas was in her life. Jax wasn't.

All they needed to do was sort out whatever had given her groom a case of cold feet.

They walked across the porch, their steps loud on the wood floor. After she pushed open the B&B's side door, she stepped into the kitchen and found Quinn in a lip-lock with Wilder.

Her gasp sent the two of them springing away from each other.

Wilder ran one hand through his hair and down to the back of his neck. He didn't look repentant in the least.

Quinn had gone peony pink, her eyes darting away from Claire's. Unfortunately, she looked right behind Claire. To Jax, of course, though Claire didn't look to see him. She could *feel* him there.

"What are *you* doing here?" Quinn demanded.

"How you doing, Quinn? You know, I've been getting that question all day." Jax's hand settled on Claire's hip, his touch warm through the thin layer of the scrubs she wore. He gave her a gentle nudge, and she stepped further in and glanced back.

He shut the door against the June bugs that rattled against the ceiling.

She wrangled her wadded up dress. Her skin scalded where his hand had been. Not good.

Wilder and Jax were doing some kind of stare-down. In her peripheral vision, Claire saw Jax give one of those chin-jerks that only a man could pull off. Wilder's eyes narrowed on him. "Aren't you that baseball guy?"

Rookie of the year, Dad had predicted. It seemed Jax was getting everything he'd wanted.

"Can I talk to you?" Quinn hissed. She took Claire's elbow and marched her down the hallway, away from the stairs that Claire desperately wanted to take up to her room.

"What is *he* doing here? Where have you been? You just disappeared! Please tell me he's not the reason Nicholas ran off this morning."

Claire's jaw dropped at the accusation. "What? No! He has nothing to do with anything."

Quinn was shooting daggers over Claire's shoulder. Claire could hear the two men talking quietly behind her.

Quinn focused back on her, genuine concern in

her expression.

Claire wilted against the wood-paneled wall. "I don't know why Nicholas left. Have you seen him at all?"

Quinn shook her head, eyes serious. "Wilder and I looked for him earlier. We tried to ask around as covertly as possible, but I don't think we fooled anyone. Then you disappeared, too, and we had to tell the guests something."

Claire closed her eyes briefly, pained. "Tell me."

"We just said there wasn't going to be a wedding today and sent them home. There was a lot of murmuring, people asking questions, and I'm sure word is already around town."

Yeah, she knew.

"Is your dad all right? Why didn't you call me?" Quinn squeezed Claire's hand.

Exhaustion was crashing over her after such an emotional day. She rubbed her temple with one hand. "I didn't have my phone. And I couldn't remember your new number. He's okay. They're keeping him overnight."

"Are you all right?" Quinn asked, aiming another glance at Jax. "Are you sure he had nothing to do with today?"

"He had nothing to do with Nicholas disappear-

ing. He showed up and helped me with Dad. And..."
She shrugged. Jax had waited for her in the ER.
Brought her food. Taken care of her.

She didn't know what she was doing.

"I need to find Nicholas," she said, her voice
weary. "And change clothes. And get my phone. Do
you know where Shelby is?"

Quinn bit her lip. Something had happened with
Shelby?

Claire narrowed her eyes at her friend.

"She, ah... caused a bit of a scene earlier. Just
before Wilder told everyone that there wasn't going
to be a wedding. I know she promised not to... it was
embarrassing. For her."

She had promised. Nicholas's sister was five
years younger than Claire, but they'd always hit it
off, even if Claire didn't understand her penchant
for the spotlight. Wasn't being an up-and-coming
music star enough? Claire had felt sure something
had changed for Shelby in the past few weeks. She'd
arrived for the rehearsal quiet and subdued, and
she'd taken Nicholas and Claire aside to assure them
there would be no drama during their wedding
weekend.

"Do you know if she's still here?" The bridal party
had rooms reserved for the entire weekend.

"I think she left," Quinn said. "I'm not sure if she was going back to her mom's place or heading out for good."

Nicholas's mother's home was the first place Claire intended to start looking. If Shelby was there, Nicholas might be, too. Or maybe the girl would know where her brother was. "Wilder hasn't heard anything from Nicholas?" The two brothers had never been that close, but if anyone could track him down, it was Wilder.

Quinn shook her head. "He's left several voice-mails, but..."

But Nicholas didn't want to be found.

Claire glanced over her shoulder, avoiding Jax's gaze for now. She couldn't help but notice that Wilder couldn't keep his eyes off of Quinn.

She turned back to her friend. "Are you sure you know what *you're* doing?" she asked, her voice low.

A blush spread up her friend's face. "No!" Quinn whispered emphatically. "We were *pretending* and then we *weren't* and now..." She shrugged, but her face was lit from within.

Claire clasped Quinn's hands and gave them a squeeze. "I'm happy for you." At least she could still feel that, when her other emotions seemed to have gone numb.

"I'll help you search for Nicholas," Quinn said. "I can catch up with Wilder later."

Claire squeezed her friend's hands and let go. Another quick look over her shoulder showed Wilder's eyes, hungry for Quinn.

Quinn deserved some happiness after the debacle with her ex. Besides, Claire wasn't even sure if she *could* find Nicholas. But she had to try. "I'm good. I'm going upstairs to get my phone. I'll call if I need you."

She slipped upstairs with only a quick wave at Jax. It'd be for the best if he left. Having him here put her off-kilter.

Upstairs, she slipped into her room, and tears pricked the back of her eyes at all the pre-wedding detritus strewn around. Her suitcase was wide open next to the bed, holding the clothes she'd taken off this morning just before she'd donned the special robe with *bride* embroidered across one shoulder. The robe lay across the end of the bed, where she'd tossed it when, with Quinn's help, she'd stepped into her wedding dress. Makeup, bobby pins, hair spray canisters... There was her phone. She moved toward the long, low dresser, avoiding her reflection in the mirror.

She'd been avoiding mirrors ever since she'd gotten Nicholas's note. Maybe it was time.

Pressing her fingers against the cool surface of the dresser, she forced her chin up, forced her eyes to meet her own gaze.

Funny. She didn't *look* like the train wreck she felt inside.

She just looked... tired. Exhaustion lined her mouth, and the hair that had been so artfully arranged in a knot behind her head was now drooping.

Avoiding her phone for the moment, she reached up and started taking pins out. One, two... faster and faster until her hair was cascading around her shoulders, wavy from the copious amounts of hairspray they'd used to secure it.

There was the Claire she'd expected to see. The Plain Jane who needed dresses to prove her femininity and kept her from wearing the jeans she loved.

Was that why Nicholas had abandoned her? Because he'd seen beyond her pretense?

She hadn't been enough to keep Jax's interest, either. Or her dad's.

Her dad had walked out on their family when Claire had been twelve. She'd never gotten over that wound. Never stopped wondering why he hadn't loved her enough. All these years later, and she still wasn't sure she could forgive him. It was why their relationship was so contentious, even though she'd tried to allow him back into her life.

And Jax... When he'd walked away in favor of his baseball career, the pit she'd fallen into had echoed the refrain at her: *You're not enough, you'll never be enough. No one loves you enough to stay.*

She'd thought Nicholas was different.

But maybe... maybe it was *her.*

Maybe that inner voice was right.

The numbness she'd been using to keep all the dark thoughts away had vanished as she'd gazed on herself in the mirror.

She broke down and sobbed into her hands.

JAX KNOCKED SOFTLY on the door. When he'd first arrived early in the afternoon, he'd gotten a glimpse of Claire in the window in her wedding finery. Of course, he hadn't known it was her at the time, and the distance had been too far to see details clearly, but he judged that this had to be the right room.

She didn't answer.

He knocked again, still taking pains to be quiet. He didn't know if there were other guests on this floor, and he knew Claire was sensitive about being

SUSAN CRAWFORD & LACY WILLIAMS

seen with him on what was supposed to have been her wedding day.

He kind of hoped she'd crawled into bed and fallen asleep. It was late. She'd been drooping with exhaustion when they'd driven over in his truck. He figured the search for her missing groom could wait another day.

Of course, that was probably because he hoped she'd give up the search altogether. And decide she wanted to give him another chance.

He leaned against the door and let his head fall forward. Talk about messed up.

He hadn't been kidding when he'd told Claire he still had feelings for her. Sure, he'd had relationships since her, but nothing long-term. Her image had popped into his mind often, the memories of their time together both sweet and painful.

Seeing her again had brought everything into keen focus.

Those last weeks before he'd been drafted to the minors, Claire had been the one thing in his life that had made sense. The one bright light in a life that was as dark as midnight.

When he'd been drafted, he'd walked away from her, seeking an even brighter light. The lights of fame and fortune and success. But those lights were fickle. They came on, flicked out, and left him in more darkness than he'd ever known. Nothing had ever been able to replace the steady love he'd had with Claire.

And now, he'd promised he'd help her find Nick. Good 'ol Nick. The man she'd fallen in love with and still wanted.

Jax was an idiot.

But he couldn't leave now. He felt the door give and barely braced himself before it opened. Struggling to remain upright, he could only hope he didn't look too foolish as he came face-to-face with Claire.

She'd changed into slim jeans and a pale pink V-neck T-shirt. She'd donned a pair of brown cowboy boots. Were they the same ones that had made him notice her back on campus? Maybe.

Her eyes were red-rimmed, and the tip of her nose was pink, as if she'd lost control in the ten minutes he'd been downstairs, chatting with good 'ol Nick's brother. The guy couldn't say why Nick had bailed, but he'd given Jax a few ideas as to where to look for him.

"This can wait until tomorrow," he said quietly. "You need to get some sleep."

She smiled tightly—not a real smile at all. "I'm fine."

He should've stepped back as she crowded through the doorway to get to the hall.

She was the one who'd moved into his space. Maybe that was why he held his position.

But nothing could explain why he raised one hand and cupped her jaw.

She froze, raised wide eyes to his face as he swept his thumb across her cheek. They were only inches apart. He really wanted to close the scant space and kiss her. "You've been crying," he whispered.

That broke the spell.

She batted his hand away and side-stepped him, then closed the door with a snap. "I won't sleep anyway. Might as well track down Shelby."

The stairs and hallway below were empty, and when they were back outside, the night had cooled but not lost any of its humidity. Jax had forgotten how sticky Texas could be.

Claire was quiet as they drove across the Sawyer Creek bridge and into town again. At this rate, he'd have the entire town map memorized by morning.

Maybe it made him a jerk, but he hoped good 'ol Nick wasn't home. He hoped the guy was gone for good. And he hoped that, when she cooled off, Claire might let him pick up the pieces of her broken heart.

Not that he'd say that.

Maybe she could feel the intensity of his thoughts, because she was out of the truck before he'd shifted it into park. Halfway up the sidewalk before he'd gotten out of the truck himself.

She knocked as he came up behind her. She turned her head. "Maybe you should wait in the car."

Too late. The door was already opening. Probably whoever was in there had seen his headlights sweep across the front of the house when he'd turned in the drive.

He braced himself to come face-to-face with the man Claire claimed to be in love with, but it was a slight woman, maybe a few years younger than Claire, who stood there. Her face was blotchy, her hair hanging in her eyes.

"Shelby, is—?" Claire's question dropped off. "What happened?"

Jax was proud that Claire had it in her, after being jilted at the altar, to ask about the other woman.

Shelby waved off her concern. "Just a... a really bad wedding d-date." It might've been more convincing if her voice hadn't wobbled.

"Aw, honey. Is there anything I can do?"

It was obvious Claire cared about Shelby, but the younger woman shook her head.

"Is your mom home?" Claire asked. "Is...is Nicholas here?"

Shelby shook her head to both. "I left Mom at the B&B, and she hasn't come home yet. I haven't seen Nick since last night."

Jax saw the droop of Claire's shoulders. She'd hoped the guy would be here.

For himself, Jax breathed a sigh of relief.

"Do you mind if I come in? If his suitcase is still here, maybe I could just... I don't know. I guess I'm hoping to find something that will make all of this make sense."

"Um..." Shelby said. "Okay, I guess."

Claire stepped forward and Shelby's glance finally encompassed Jax. For the first time, she seemed to realize Claire wasn't alone.

"Who's—?"

"Just a friend." Claire shot him a look over her shoulder. She didn't seem furious with him anymore. Only resigned. "He'll wait in the car."

Dismissed.

He wanted to be upset about it, but he couldn't forget the look on her face when she'd emerged from her room. Devastated.

He trudged to his truck to wait.

CLAIRE DIDN'T KNOW what she hoped to find here. Nicholas had insisted on staying at his mother's house while the rest of the bridal party had been put up at the bed-and-breakfast.

She'd sometimes teased him that he was so tight he squeaked when he walked. She'd chalked up his desire to stay at his mom's as part of that side of his personality.

Had he been having second thoughts before they'd even booked the wedding venue?

It looked as if he'd slept on the couch last night. There was a pillow and blanket folded neatly at the end of the faded plaid monstrosity. A black garment bag that housed his tuxedo was draped over the back of the couch, zipped and pristine. Seeing it sent a pang through Claire.

His duffel bag was open on the glass-topped coffee table. A glance inside revealed perfectly ordered stacks of clothing, his socks rolled neatly on top.

What exactly had she thought she'd find by coming here? Some written list of reasons he'd decided to dump her on the day of their wedding? Or maybe a hand-drawn map with a bullseye showing where she could find him? Or, better yet, a pros-and-cons list of whether he should marry her.

Pro... *she's already planned the whole shindig.* Con... *I don't love her and never have.*

She shook off the thought. Sank onto the couch, exhausted. Her hands covered her face, and she wanted to weep all over again.

What was the point? Even if she found Nicholas, and even if he did have a good excuse—she couldn't imagine one that was remotely good enough—it didn't mean she could ever trust him again.

Someone who truly loved her wouldn't have left her at the altar with a note.

What did that say about her, that she hadn't noticed her fiancé was unhappy? She'd been busy with the wedding preparations for months, plus checking in on her father, boxing up her entire apartment, saying goodbyes at her old job.

Still, she should've noticed.

She exhaled loudly, dropping her hands from her face.

Several magazines were spread across the coffee table. One was a sports magazine, and on the cover... Jax. She couldn't escape from him if she tried.

She'd been studiously ignoring the billboards that seemed to appear everywhere she looked, his face plastered every few miles for the entire state to see.

Quinn had been kind enough not to bring up the

fact that her ex was coming back to Texas. Claire had just wanted to ignore it.

But... What was this magazine doing here? Had it been a coincidence that it was on Mrs. Caine's table? Maybe it belonged to Wilder. Claire glanced to see if there was a subscription address label on it. There wasn't. Which meant someone had bought it at a newsstand.

Did it belong to Nicholas?

She didn't like the direction her thoughts were going.

If this magazine belonged to Nicholas, did that mean he'd been thinking about Jax? Worrying about how she felt about him?

When she and Nicholas had gotten serious, she'd told him about her dating history, including Jax. Not all of it, but enough that he knew she'd been broken-hearted when Jax had walked away.

Had Nicholas worried because she *hadn't* brought up Jax's return? And if he had, why hadn't he just talked to her? She could've reassured him that Jax meant nothing to her.

Except...

Except.

When she'd seen Jax, she'd had an instant reaction. She'd thought it was anger—she'd *slapped* him!

—but if she had truly been over him, would she have had reason to get so angry?

She stood, cutting off the train of her thoughts.

No. She didn't have feelings for Jax. Not any longer.

She walked through the house to the front door. "Shelby, I'm heading out!" she called.

Shelby returned an, "Okay!" from somewhere deeper in the house. There'd been obvious signs that the girl was upset, but she hadn't wanted to talk. Claire could only hope her outburst at the bed-and-breakfast hadn't created bad press for the musician.

Claire got into Jax's truck.

He turned his head on the headrest. Looked at her. "Hey."

She told herself to shut the door and not look at him.

But her stomach had done a slow flip at the warmth in his tone.

She was immune to him.

Except she wasn't.

"You're wiped," he said.

She glanced at the clock on the dash. After midnight. The day from hell had officially ended, but nothing was resolved.

"You want me to drive you back to your dad's? If

you crash for a few hours, we can be back at it fairly early."

"Yeah. That's a good idea." The last place she wanted to stay was at her dad's, but she needed to check on the dog, and she was exhausted.

What she really needed was to send Jax on his way. All he'd done was stir up things that were better left settled.

CHAPTER 4

*J*ax figured Claire would jump right out of the truck when he pulled into the drive at her dad's house. That's what she'd done when he'd pulled into Shelby's drive.

But she didn't.

One hand fisted on her jean-clad thigh, she stared out the window. Was she waiting for him to say something? Walk her inside?

"What was it like, living in New York?" she asked the window.

It was so unexpected that he sat there for long seconds, sure his ears were playing tricks on him. "My apartment was in Jersey. It was... different."

He turned the key, and the engine died, leaving

them in silence interrupted only by the ticking of the cooling engine.

"Different how?"

Did she really care? He would hate to misuse this opportunity if she were open to having a real conversation with him.

You weren't there. He couldn't say that, so he said, "It was lonely at first. It took a while for me to make friends." Some of the players were so competitive—even against their teammates—that the locker room was often tense. "Some things didn't change. Workouts. Nutrition."

The biggest difference had been that he'd only had one job, instead of the three he'd carried during college. Pay wasn't great in the minor leagues, but it was better than what he'd had before. He'd made it work. The extra hours in his day had been put to use with more workout time, watching tapes, and pitching practice.

"I still remember the first game I played. The pitching coach told me to warm up, and I had to run for the bathroom." He'd gotten violently sick, nerves threatening to ruin his big chance. Thankfully, after he'd emptied the contents of his stomach, he'd been able to get into the rhythm of throwing pitches in the bullpen, and he'd been able to overcome the nerves.

Was she smiling? Without the dash lights illuminating the truck's interior, there was no reflection in the passenger window. And he had only the barest glimpse of the side of her mouth. He couldn't tell.

"Was it scary, moving up there when you didn't know anyone?"

"I don't know. Not really." There weren't many things scarier than being nine years old and not knowing where your next meal was coming from. Not knowing if your dad was coming home that night. Not knowing if you could trust the people who were supposed to help you—teachers, cops. After surviving the hole he'd crawled out of, not much scared him. He worked hard, harder than anyone else he knew. And it was finally paying off.

"Did you have any relationships? I'm sure a lot of girls chase after famous baseball players."

"I'm not famous."

Her head angled toward him, and there was no mistaking the roll of her eyes. She arched one brow, waiting.

"There were a couple of relationships. Nothing meaningful." There'd always been something missing. He'd attributed it to his busy schedule, or that it just wasn't the right fit.

But all along, he'd been missing Claire.

He turned the tables on her. "How long have you and Nick been together?"

She let her head fall against the seat back. "Two and a half years."

Ouch. She hadn't waited long after he'd left to date again.

"We got engaged four months ago. We were going to get married this Christmas, but when my dad got diagnosed, Nicholas agreed that we should move up the wedding."

"How'd you get back in touch with your dad?" Last Jax knew, she hadn't seen the guy since he'd walked out on her and her mom.

"Nicholas encouraged me to patch things up. Dad had been calling and leaving me messages saying he wanted to talk, and..." A pause, as if her mind had wandered off somewhere. "Nicholas said that holding onto bitterness would make me unhappy in the long run."

Yeah, but allowing someone back into your life who was Kryptonite could do major damage.

As if his own bitter thoughts had prompted the

action from two hundred miles away, Jax's phone screen lit up with an incoming call. After midnight. Because his dad was considerate like that. What if Jax had been sleeping?

He sent the call to voicemail and flipped the phone over on the bench seat between them. He'd deal with his dad later. Or never.

"So Nick asked you to make up with your dad. And then he asked you to... quit your job and move back here?"

Her eyes narrowed, and he shrugged. "Your friend Wilder mentioned it."

Back at the B&B, Wilder had been a mix of impressed and suspicious. They'd only chatted for a few minutes, but Jax had latched onto the mention of Claire's job.

"It's a long commute to Austin," she said quietly. Almost as if she were repeating something that had been said to her.

"I liked my job at the Children's Hospital." She spoke with a note of defiance.

"I bet you were good at it." When they'd been together, it had been easy to imagine her as a pediatric nurse. She loved kids.

He'd also imagined the two of them having a

houseful. Not that he'd know what to do with a kid. He'd had the worst example in the history of fatherhood. Still, with Claire, he'd had the nerve to dream.

Remembering that brought a flood of acid to his gut. He'd let it go—or he thought he had—when he'd left Claire behind.

The ache in his chest was the only thing he could blame for the next words out of his mouth. "Do you ever wonder? You know... what if?"

What if he'd chosen differently? What if he'd asked her to go with him?

She stared out the windshield, the blanket of stars visible above the roof of her dad's place. "No."

Her single word was a pitch straight to the ribcage. Made it hard to breathe.

Until he repeated it in his head and heard the slightest edge of uncertainty in her voice.

CLAIRE WOKE DISORIENTED, and she had a crick in her neck. Also, her entire left leg was asleep.

She shifted, and the man she was snuggled up to grunted in protest.

Wha—?

Oh. She was married to Nicholas, and they were on their honeymoon.

She pried open her eyes, blinking through the still-lingering disorientation.

The gray light of dawn seeped in through windows on all sides—because she wasn't married to Nicholas, and she wasn't on her honeymoon.

She'd fallen asleep in Jax's truck.

Real memories surged to the forefront of her brain, replacing her sleep-fogged dream-induced ones. Nicholas. Sawyer Creek. Jax.

With a gasp, she pushed off his chest, where she'd pillowed her head sometime in the night. His muscled arm fell away—he'd been *holding* her in his sleep—and he shifted, coming awake as he groaned and straightened in the driver's seat.

She hadn't meant to fall asleep in his truck at all. They'd started talking, and after things had gotten deeply serious, their conversation had turned lighter. And they'd kept talking... And that's all she remembered.

That didn't explain how she'd ended up in the middle of the bench seat, or why she'd been cozied up to her ex.

She rubbed both hands over her eyes. Tried to erase the images of his sleep-relaxed face.

She peered through her fingers to find his lips turned up in a lazy smile, his eyes soft. "Morning."

Shaken, she couldn't find words. And then, they came. "Did you do this on purpose?" She craned her neck to look down the street both ways. No traffic. She could be grateful for small favors, but that didn't mean... "Anyone who drove by could've seen us!"

Her words were too high, too filled with emotion. But she couldn't call them back.

His easy smile faded. "No one drove by."

"How do you know?" She'd been asleep. They both had. She couldn't be sure no one had seen them during the night.

"The whole town was rolling up its sidewalks at nine o'clock. I doubt anyone on this street was out later than we were. And it's not even dawn now."

She hated that he could be reasonable when all she felt was acute panic building in her chest. She didn't know what her life was going to look like now. Where things would end up with Nicholas. But if she had any hope of salvaging that relationship, if word got out that she'd stayed out all night with Jax... She shivered. She didn't want to think about what Nicholas would think about that.

And she also hated how safe and comfortable she'd felt wrapped in Jax's arms. His smell was seared into her nostrils. He still used the same soap.

She'd scrubbed it from her memory banks once, but now the scent clung, breaking open the wall of memories she'd once painstakingly bricked over.

She pressed shaking fingers to the bridge of her nose. What was she supposed to do now? She was so turned around, she didn't know the right thing.

"You're trying to sabotage my relationship with Nicholas," she said, the words emerging before she'd really consciously thought them.

"What relationship?" His tone carried an edge. "He *left* you."

The words were a blow, one that struck true. Nicholas had walked away on what was supposed to be their wedding day.

But… "You left me, too." She reached for the door handle blindly, fumbling with the electronic locks. "This was a mistake, leaning on you for help."

"Claire, wait."

She wouldn't listen to him anymore. No doubt he'd have some smooth-talking way to keep her in the truck, to keep her close.

So that... what? So he could hurt her all over again when he left for Dallas?

"You should go back to your baseball team," she said, finally getting the door open.

"Baseball wasn't the only reason I left."

She froze, her gaze darting to his face at the unexpected words. She was really shaking now. Not sure whether she really wanted to hear what he had to say.

"Enlighten me, then." She'd meant the words to snap, but her voice was shaky instead. "Maybe I can learn why I keep driving the men in my life away."

He frowned. "It's not like that." He looked out the front windshield, away from her. "It wasn't about you at all. I left because of—because you didn't really know me. And if I let you get any closer, I knew you'd start to see the real me."

She was confused. They'd told each other everything back then, hadn't they? "What are you talking about?"

He glanced at her, at her hand on the still-open door. Maybe he was trying to decide if she was getting ready to jump out of the truck. She *should* get out. Get far, far away from him before he could convince her to stay.

His frown deepened as if he could read her mind. He'd always been able to sense her mood.

"Claire, I came from nothing."

His words made no sense.

"Didn't you ever wonder why I never invited you to my apartment?"

She hadn't. Not really. "I thought you were trying to be gentlemanly. Not pressure me to be physical." She'd lived in a dorm with her homebody of a room-mate—at her place they'd been limited to goodnight kisses.

His smile was twisted. Wrong, somehow. "I didn't want you to see the real me. I slept on the floor until about a month before I met you, when I could finally afford a mattress. Not a bed frame, or even a box spring. Just a mattress on the floor. And a used one at that. I didn't have a TV, no furniture. But I was lucky to eat three meals a day, even if most of them were rice and beans."

The early morning humidity had filled the truck. She should close the door. She still wasn't sure, though, if she should be on the other side of the door when she did. Compassion filled her for the college kid he was describing. That wasn't how she remembered it at all. "You worked so hard."

"Harder than you knew. I had three jobs so I could string together enough hours around the base-ball schedule to make rent and buy food."

He'd never told her that. She'd known he worked at a coffee shop on campus, and she'd never questioned it further when he'd claimed to have to work through the evening on a weeknight.

"Working hard isn't something to be ashamed of," she said. "You should be proud of what you've made of yourself."

There was still a darkness, a bleakness in his eyes. There was more. What more?

I came from nothing.

Did he mean more than poverty?

JAX DIDN'T KNOW if he could do this.

He didn't even know how he'd gotten here. He'd come to Sawyer Creek yesterday to track down Claire, and now he was spilling secrets he'd once left to protect.

But she still had that hand on the door. She was one step away from walking away from him forever.

He would never forget the look of utter despair that had crossed her face just a few moments before —*maybe I can learn why I keep driving the men in my life away.*

He hated that he'd made her feel defective when he'd walked away. The reality was, he'd been a coward.

He had to do this.

But he couldn't look at her. He focused on a pot of red geraniums on her dad's neighbor's porch.

"Your dad walked out when you were twelve," he said. "Mine walked when I was two. The only difference was, he never left."

He hated thinking back to that time in his childhood. He hadn't known anything different until elementary school, when he'd realized not every kid got slapped around by their old man. Other kids had moms who came to sit with them during the school lunch period. Other kids' dads weren't despicable.

"My old man was... pretty mean." Understatement of the year. "He used to knock me around. Until I was a teenager." That's when Jax had started mouthing off, threatening to call the cops on his dad. Not that it had done any good. Turned out his dad was a lot better at threats than Jax. He'd lived in a state of perpetual fear until he'd run away.

Claire made a soft noise, but Jax still couldn't look at her. If he stopped talking now, he'd never start up again. "He was... mixed up in some bad stuff. Dangerous stuff." Drugs, women, booze, guns.

"I left when I was sixteen. I was tall enough, and my beard had already started coming in." He scraped one hand along the stubble at his jaw "I found this homeless shelter and lied about my age. They let me stay there while I figured things out."

An ache pounded behind his eyes, but he needed to get through this.

"While I was there, this one guy who volunteered helped me get some textbooks. I got my GED. He helped me find work, and I started saving up for my first month's rent. And then I got that crappy apartment and got in to junior college, and..." And met Claire. He'd made her coffee ten times before he'd gotten up the courage to ask her out.

Before he'd met her, baseball had been the best thing about his life. He'd played in junior high and high school, until he'd run away, and his sophomore coach had seen something in him. Had worked with him. Then he'd had no way to play while his life had fallen apart. When he'd walked on the junior college team and found his skill hadn't left him, it was like a gift from above. Baseball was the only thing that made sense. Baseball didn't judge. The fans didn't care where he came from or what kind of life he'd lived. So he made baseball his life.

Until Claire. The months they'd been together— as often as his work schedule and games had allowed —had been the best thing in his life.

"And then I started getting some interest from

scouts. And my dad started calling me." He laughed bitterly. "He's always been able to sniff out a paycheck."

"But he didn't have anything to do with you," she said softly. She was still on the precipice. Halfway out the door.

Jax shook his head. "You don't know my dad. I told you he was dangerous. He had a long reach. Connections to crooks everywhere. You asked me last night if I was scared to move across the country. I wasn't. I was glad." He took a breath. "There were a lot of times I wished him dead—wished a deal would go wrong and he'd be on the wrong end of a bullet. Sometimes I still do."

There was a long beat of silence. He couldn't look at her. He didn't want to see the censure—or worse, the pity—in her expression.

Finally, she spoke. "So that's it? That's your big secret? That's why you broke up with me?"

Surprised by the sarcasm, he snapped his gaze to hers. Her eyes were sharp, angry.

He shook his head. He'd known he was going to mess this up. "I didn't want... There's this whole ugly side of me." He gripped the steering wheel until his knuckles went white. "And I never wanted you to see any of it. You came from this other life and..." Back

77

then, he'd been so afraid that she'd see the real him and reject him.

And maybe he hadn't grown up that much, because right now, he'd do or say anything to keep her from walking away.

His phone buzzed again. The worst timing ever.

He tapped the screen to reject the call, and it went dark.

She grabbed the device out of his hands. "Who keeps calling you?"

He shook his head.

She tapped a few times on the screen, but she wouldn't find a name for that number in his contacts list. He didn't even know how his old man had gotten the number. Didn't need to know.

"This same number has called you forty-five times in the last week." Her nose was almost pressed to his phone.

He huffed out a breath. She wasn't going to leave it alone.

"It's him," he said. "He left me some messages. He got sent to prison about a year after I ran away. Now he claims he's got cancer. And religion. And he wants to see me before he dies."

Her gaze met his. "Aren't you the least bit curious?"

"Nope. It's been all over the place that I made the majors. He knows I have money now. That's all he cares about."

And Jax had promised himself when he crawled out of his old life that he was never going back.

CHAPTER 5

*H*ow in the heck had he ended up here?

Jax stared at the squat brick building surrounded by chain link fence topped with razor wire. The prison where his dad was supposedly in the sick bay. Dying.

If you could believe someone for whom lying was second nature.

He didn't want to go in there.

A cool hand met his palm, fingers twining around his.

He looked down at Claire. She was how he'd gotten here.

He knew she didn't harbor romantic feelings toward him anymore. At least he didn't think so. She meant the hand-holding as a friendly gesture, and he was glad to have her beside him.

He was still hanging on to that one-in-a-million chance that he could win her back. This was part of it.

She'd been angry, hurt that he hadn't let her know all of him. Well, this visit would cure that. Once they went inside and saw his dad, she'd know the ugliness that he'd been born from. She'd understand why he'd hidden it from her.

He forced his feet to move. There were no trees around the place—probably as a measure to keep inmates from escape—and by the time they'd crossed the parking lot, Jax was sweating through his T-shirt.

The glass door was plastered with warnings. No firearms, no knives, no contraband. And on and on.

Real welcoming place.

Inside, the linoleum floor was old and cracked. A uniformed guard sat on a stool behind a glass partition. Jax headed there.

It took a good half hour for them to sign in, go through metal detectors, and then be escorted through an iron-barred gate and down a long, dim corridor.

The gate clanged closed behind them, and Jax

couldn't help looking over his shoulder. All of a sudden, he couldn't breathe. He was trapped in here. The guards had cut off any escape.

At his side, Claire squeezed his hand.

He took a stuttering breath and told himself to stop being so dramatic.

The antiseptic smell hit him first. It smelled like a hospital. They were led into a room that stretched nearly the length from home plate to right field. It was lined with curtained cubicles. The few they could see into were empty.

At the end of the cubicles was another room that had a large viewing window. Inside, a man in scrubs was holding a clipboard, his attention fixed on a shelf beside him.

Everything was sterile. Cold.

The guard pointed them to the last cubicle. Jax felt like he was swimming through concrete. Even the noise around him seemed muted, as though he were underwater.

He could still turn around.

But he pressed on.

As he neared the cubicle, Claire hung back, her hand pulling back on his. Her fingers went lax.

He tugged her forward. She'd insisted he come. She might as well see all the ugliness.

Jax looked down at the hospital bed and the man who lay there. His dad was asleep. He had oxygen tubes in his nose, and several softly-beeping monitors showing his vital signs.

He looked so *old*. He'd lost his hair, and his face was etched with deep lines.

Had he always been that small? He was nothing like the monstrous villain in Jax's memories.

Jax stood there in shock. Stared in silence for far too long.

His father really was dying.

The man came out of the glass-window room. As he bustled into the cubicle, Jax saw the RN on his ID badge. "Let's see if he'll wake up. Hate to waste your visit without talking to him."

Jax cleared his throat, surprised to find his voice rough. "What's wrong with him?"

The nurse checked a bag of clear liquid hooked to the IV stand. "Heard him leave a voicemail for you. It's cancer. Late stage. Glad you didn't wait any longer. You might've missed him."

Cancer. So it really was the end.

His father roused with a groan. "What?" he growled, and while the voice was weaker, it was the same voice from Jax's nightmares.

The nurse was unfazed. "You've got visitors."

It took his father several seconds to focus on Jax. He'd woken with an aura of pain in his expression, but when he realized who was standing there, his face smoothed as clear as a pane of glass.

"You finally showed up," the old man said. "Decided to pay your final respects after all?"

There was nothing to respect in the man in front of him. Jax didn't say a word.

CLAIRE FELT like she was watching a train wreck in slow motion. Helpless to stop what was happening, even though she wanted to.

Jax's dad coughed, the sound wet and weak.

She'd never met anyone with eyes like his. They were a pale blue, but it wasn't the color that made her unable to look away. She felt... transfixed at the absolute cold, deadness inside.

"Read about you in the newspaper," the older man said. "Kinda thought my own flesh and blood would've called to let me know he was coming home."

I don't have a home.

Jax had played off the statement—had it only been yesterday?—pretending he'd meant he was house-shopping, but that hadn't been it at all. Today, he'd flayed himself open and showed her the beating heart inside his chest.

He'd brought her here to meet the father who had *knocked him around*. And probably worse. Who hadn't given him a home.

Jax had been searching for one ever since.

This train wreck was all her fault.

Up to this point, Jax hadn't said a word, but it seemed he'd finally found his voice. "We might have blood ties, but we've never been a family."

The old man's lips twisted in an ugly grimace. "Hear you're rakin' in the big bucks now that you're in the bigs. You might think your money can buy you a new life, put some distance between what you come from. But blood always outs."

Jax was fairly vibrating with tension beside her.

Whatever she'd hoped this visit with his dad would solve for Jax, this wasn't it. She'd listened to his story and judged it against her own past. Had thought that his dad must want reconciliation if he'd called Jax so many times.

Obviously, she'd been wrong.

She tugged on Jax's hand. "C'mon."

She wasn't going to let the man in that bed hurt him any longer.

Jax looked down at her as if he'd forgotten her

presence entirely. But he let her pull him away from the cubicle, down the hall, back to where the guard stood ready to escort them out of the prison.

Jax was silent, the clatter of their footsteps on the tile floor the only sound as they retraced their steps.

They collected her purse, his wallet, their cell phones, and his keys from the front counter where they'd been required to leave them. Then, they stepped out into the sunlight that seemed harsh after the dim interior.

Jax silently trudged across the parking lot and opened the passenger door for her.

She was about to apologize when her cell phone rang. The wedding march played. Nicholas's special ringtone.

She dug for the phone, not sure whether she intended to silence it or answer it.

It continued ringing in her hand as she looked into Jax's face. He wore a sad smile, one that was both resigned and bitter. "You'd better answer that."

CHAPTER 6

*N*icholas had asked her to meet at the gazebo back at the bed-and-breakfast.

She wasn't sure whether that was a hopeful sign or a bittersweet one.

At this point, she wasn't sure she deserved to hope for reconciliation. She'd jumped back into...something—not friendship, something more—with Jax before she'd even shed her wedding gown.

Maybe she was the one who didn't deserve Nicholas.

Jax let her off at the front porch of the B&B. He didn't ask her for a promise—or even a phone number. He didn't say goodbye. He just drove off in a swirl of gravel dust.

Nicholas was already in the gazebo when she

made her way across the artfully manicured lawn. He stood with his back to her, looking out toward the undeveloped woods at the back of the property.

When she stepped up into the structure, he turned to face her. His hands were in his pockets. He looked as if he hadn't slept since she'd seen him last at the rehearsal. His eyes were bloodshot and his hair rumpled. She'd seen him run his hands through it when he was worried or tense. How many times had his fingers traced the pattern since he'd left her the day before?

"Hey." She hung back, wrapped one arm around one of the gazebo pillars.

"Hey."

This felt... incredibly awkward. Was she supposed to hug him? She was glad to see him, even if her heart hadn't slammed against her ribs the way it had when she'd seen Jax for the first time in three years.

"Are you okay?" she asked.

He nodded. Then shook his head. "I don't... I'm so sorry. I should've... should've done a lot of things."

She gripped the post, hard. "If you were having second thoughts, why didn't you talk to me?"

He rolled his shoulders, a sign of his discomfort. "Because... it was stupid. I kept thinking that if we went through with it, everything would be fine.

Once we were married, I could make you happy enough that you wouldn't..." He swallowed hard. "But when it came down to the wire, I just... I knew you still had feelings for him."

She didn't have to ask who the *him* was. *Oh, Nicholas.*

He looked as miserable as she felt. "If you had accused me of that two days ago, I would've laughed in your face, but..."

But.

The last thirty-six hours had made her question everything. And Jax showing up out of the blue had been a big part of it.

She sat heavily on a bench built into the gazebo. "If you asked me today, I don't know what my answer would be."

She hated herself for being so weak-minded.

They remained in silence for a long stretch.

"When we first started dating, you didn't want to talk about him at all," Nicholas said. "And I was so infatuated with you, I didn't care. But the longer we were together... I kept thinking you'd finally let me in, but you kept your broken heart to yourself."

He was right. She'd been afraid to re-open the wounds she'd received when Jax had broken up with her. Afraid of what it meant if they weren't healed.

This wedding fiasco was as much her fault as it was Nicholas's.

She sniffled back the tears that threatened. "And then I wanted to push up the wedding because of my dad."

He nodded. "And I went along with it."

She needed him to know. "If we had gotten married, I never would've been unfaithful to you."

She didn't see how he could believe her, not when she'd run right out and spent most of the last day with Jax. She'd even fallen asleep in his embrace.

But he was nodding. "No, but he would've always had first place in your heart. I've never been good at being second place. Just ask Wilder."

"You should be first place," she whispered through a throat choked with tears. Nicholas had been good to her. He'd pulled her out of that dark place, helped her reunite with her dad. He was a good man.

But he wasn't Jax. He wasn't the man who'd made her believe in love in the first place. The man who'd faced down his demons because she'd demanded it. The man who'd captured her heart and never given it back.

A tear slipped free. "I'm sorry, too."

Claire didn't know where to go from here. She'd

built her life around Nicholas, around a marriage that was never going to happen. How did she go on?

"Maybe it's time for you to chase him," Nicholas said, as if he'd followed the trajectory of her thoughts.

She looked at him. Really looked at him. Saw the sincere love in his eyes. Saw that he was letting her go.

"It's okay," he said. "I'll be okay."

But she didn't know if she would. Did she deserve Jax's love after everything that had happened, then and now?

HE SHOULD'VE GONE BACK to Dallas.

Instead, Jax found himself out in the boonies under a canopy of scrub oaks on the bank of Sawyer Creek.

Because he was just that pitiful.

At least the combination of the trees, the late afternoon breeze, and the fact that the sun was setting gave him some relief from the day's heat.

Too bad there was no relief for his heart.

He'd finally figured it out, after all this time.

Claire was his home. His touchstone. The reason he'd never been able to forget Texas, not completely.

SUSAN CRAWFORD & LACY WILLIAMS

Even the aftermath of his visit with his dad was only a phantom ache. There was a time it would've left him gutted. He'd gotten through it because Claire was at his side.

But she didn't belong to him.

Blood always outs.

His father's words still rang in his head. He tried to shake them loose.

He bent and picked up a smooth stone from the ground. There'd been a turnoff—a dirt path really— just after the bridge on the way out of town. He'd parked off the road and walked down here where the creek widened. The clear water trickled over a mix of brown and silver rocks on the creek bed.

He aimed and threw. His rock skipped four times and sank heavily into the water.

He should go. Claire was with Nicholas. If the guy had smartened up at all, he'd be heading for the nearest judge and getting that ring on her finger. Like Jax should've.

A car door closed, and Jax's head whipped around.

There was Claire, picking her way through the taller grass before the woods cleared into soft dirt and half-decayed leaves.

She was so beautiful that it made him ache. She'd

changed clothes. Not into a sundress, like he might've expected. She'd always worn sundresses back then. Now, she wore jeans, a red tank top, and strappy sandals on her feet. She was breathtaking.

She looked up at him once, then back down at her feet as she navigated the bank. She put out one hand and touched the trunk of a massive elm for balance. "I saw your truck."

She sounded slightly breathless. Maybe even happy to see him. No, that was just his imagination, reaching again.

"Yeah?" Maybe if good 'ol Nick hadn't called her earlier, he'd have had some hope. But this felt suspiciously like a goodbye.

"Yeah." She stopped several feet away, too far for him to reach out and touch her. Her gaze hit his face, and he read the concern there. "What your dad said... earlier..."

Blood always outs.

He bit down on the frustrated noise that wanted to escape his throat. He couldn't look at her, not if the only reason she was here was to give him friendly comfort. He looked away, out at the water.

"It's not true. You know that, right?"

He nodded, because that's what she expected.

"Jax."

Of course she wouldn't let it go that easily. She wouldn't be the woman he loved if she would.

If this was the end, better to face it. He turned his gaze back to her. The fierce conviction in her expression made his gut twist. Made him want to beg her not to say goodbye.

"It's not true," she repeated.

"My head wants to believe it." He touched his brow, then his heart. "But here..." He exhaled. Shook his head.

She took a step toward him. "Then maybe..." A deep breath. "I'll have to believe it for you. Until you start to believe it, too."

His heart pounded as wild hope crashed through him. Because that sounded like...

He didn't dare think it.

He bent and picked up another smooth stone. Turned away from her to the creek.

She stepped beside him. Crouched for a moment, and then straightened.

"If you're talking about being friends, that's never going to be enough for me." He flung the rock, watched it skip three times and sink. "I want more."

She said nothing for a long time as he squinted at the shadows on the water's surface. Long enough for him to regret the blunt honesty.

She tossed her rock, and he counted the skips. Eight. Nine. Ten. It slipped into the water with a soft *ploop.*

"I always wanted to come here," he said. "You told me about Sawyer Creek once. About the time before your mom and dad split, and I was just... jealous. It sounded like heaven."

In his periphery, he saw her tilt her head back to take in the sky darkening above the treetops. When she said nothing, he added, "It kind of is, isn't it?"

Her silence on the subject was telling.

If this was goodbye, he wanted it to be over.

She turned toward him, and he couldn't help the force of gravity that pulled his body to mirror hers.

Her eyes were soft and luminous as she looked up at him. "Friendship would never be enough for me either."

The breath he'd inhaled was now lodged in his chest, so tight he started to feel lightheaded. "Are you saying...? Claire, I want to be with you. Still. Always. I love you."

Saying the words, putting it out there, made him uneasy. When they'd dated in college, she'd been the one to say it first, allowing him the security of knowing she returned his feelings before he'd had to commit to them.

But after all this, didn't she deserve to hear it first?

Her eyes fluttered closed, then squeezed tight, and he dared to take the half-step to close the distance between them. He took both her hands in his, twining their fingers together.

"I want to try," she whispered. "To be together again."

He brushed a kiss to her cheek, then touched his forehead to hers.

"I don't know if the trust that was broken between us can be rebuilt," she confessed softly.

That was a hit, but he squeezed her hands gently. "You'll never know how sorry I am that I let you go."

Her eyes opened, and she gazed at him. He tried to send her silent promises that he wouldn't let her down again, that he'd be everything she needed— even if it meant turning himself inside out.

"And Nicholas?" he asked.

She shook her head slightly. "Turns out, he was the one who realized I still had feelings for you. That's why..."

Huh. Maybe the guy wasn't such a jerk after all. Jax would've taken the selfish road and stolen her away, but good 'ol Nick had set her free.

Her expression was vulnerable, open. "Can we take things slowly?"

He nodded, their foreheads bumping gently. Anything. He'd give her anything she wanted.

Jax let go of one of her hands and cupped her jaw. "Can I please kiss you? For a day and a half, I've been dying to."

A slow smile spread across her lips, and he took that for his answer, dropping his head to join their lips.

He'd been right. Kissing her was like coming home.

CHAPTER 7

THREE MONTHS LATER

*C*laire let her gaze swing around the interior of the Dallas Coyotes' home stadium. Since she and Jax had agreed to rebuild their relationship, she'd watched numerous home games. Usually from the special box two levels up, the one reserved for team spouses and girlfriends.

But today, Jax had asked her to sit in the stands. She hadn't realized the ticket he'd had couriered to her would put her on the second row, just behind the catcher.

She'd jumped twice when her attention had

wandered and the ball had *thwacked* forcefully into the catcher's mitt.

Jax had started the game. Six innings in, he was still in the zone and throwing well. He'd been utterly focused on the game, even though he had to be able to see her from this close.

She was trying to make herself as small as possible. She didn't want to break his concentration.

She loved watching him play. He'd been focused in college, more so than any of his teammates. But this was another level.

He played as if he were still proving himself.

Her dad's prediction had come true. Jax was nearing the end of his first season in the majors, and there was constant media buzz about him being a contender for Rookie of the Year. His ERA was the third best in the league.

He couldn't walk down the street without fans flocking around him, including tons of women.

But his attention never wavered from Claire. Not once.

Her dad had passed away two months ago. Jax had been by her side the entire time, even taking an approved absence from a couple of games. In the end, she'd been able to forgive him for his desertion. And he'd been in such pain those last few weeks that she had been relieved when he passed. Her grief still caught her unaware sometimes, but she was incandescently happy with Jax.

Without anything tying her to Sawyer Creek, she'd decided to take a job at the Children's Hospital in Dallas. Being closer to Jax meant seeing more of him. Much more. Even so, he was frequently away for days at a time.

She'd worn out her phone's battery taking his constant video calls. And working with the kids she loved kept her from going stir-crazy while her famous boyfriend was gone.

Jax hadn't let her sell her dad's house. He'd wanted to keep it, to have a place they could retreat to during the off-season. He'd already been talking about going back.

She loved their time together, but between the media and his intense schedule, she couldn't wait to have some down time for them to just *be*.

Right now, the last Dallas batter was two strikes in, and then they'd have the seventh-inning stretch. She'd been waiting. She wanted to grab a Coke.

But as the pitcher wound up, a college-aged girl in a team T-shirt appeared at Claire's elbow, distracting her.

"Hey, Miss Davidson," the girl chirped. "You're supposed to come with me."

Um, what? "I'm—" Claire gestured to the game playing out before them. Except the Coyotes player had struck out, and the fielders were jogging toward the dugout.

"Boss's orders," the girl said.

Whose orders? Claire didn't know this girl.

She took Claire's arm as if she was going to physically pull her out of the seat.

"Okay, okay."

Claire gave one longing glance up the stadium stairs to her missed concession opportunity. She followed the girl, surprised when they went down instead of up, and even more surprised when the girl opened a little gate and motioned for Claire to go out on the field.

She hesitated.

And then a beefy security guard motioned her forward. "C'mon." Had he winked at her?

Claire's brain was whirling. What was going on? Was Jax hurt? He'd used a pinch-hitter, so she hadn't seen him since he'd jogged off the field at the bottom of the last inning.

The deep-voiced announcer spoke over the loudspeaker, but the words were garbled in her ears as she made her way down a narrow metal staircase.

And then the loudspeaker guy got real clear. "Stay in your seats, folks. We're forgoing the usual rendition of *Take Me Out to the Ballgame* because we've got a special treat for you. You won't want to miss this.'"

Claire froze as she caught sight of the Jumbotron on the opposite end of the field. Somewhere there was a camera pointed right at her. Zoomed in so that the perplexed expression on her face was visible for every single person in the stadium to see.

"Miss, if you please." The security guard motioned her toward the pitcher's mound.

Where Jax stood.

The rest of the field was empty.

"C'mere," he called out, his voice carrying clearly over the sixty some-odd feet to where she stood at home plate.

Her knees wobbled as she started across the green expanse toward him.

What was he doing? Was this—? There was only one reason—one *big* reason—she could imagine him making a big spectacle out of her.

The butterflies in her stomach took flight.

Jax didn't look nervous at all. He was handsome

SUSAN CRAWFORD & LACY WILLIAMS

in his home whites—the white and navy-trimmed uniform—his head bare. His hair was slightly mussed, but it just made him look more gorgeous.

Claire's swirling thoughts narrowed to a single point of focus—him—as her sandaled feet hit the pitcher's mound.

He reached for her hands and held them both loosely in his. He was shaking.

"What're you doing?" she whispered. She tried not to move her mouth, knowing that with that camera focused on her, every fan in the stadium could read her lips.

He laughed a little, his smile wry. "I'm really nervous."

His voice boomed out of the loudspeakers, and she realized someone had mic'd him. A thin black wire and tiny microphone were visible at the neckline of his jersey.

He *was* nervous.

The knowledge settled her own nerves. "It's okay," she whispered. "Ask me."

OF COURSE she'd figured it out. Claire was too smart for him to fool for long.

Jax loved her desperately. And he knew she loved him back.

Which meant popping the question should be easy.

He hadn't expected the nerves. Apparently, there was still some part of that scared boy inside who knew there was a chance she'd say no. He wanted to shut that voice up forever.

He went to one knee, still holding Claire's hands.

The crowd went wild, yelling and screaming, stomping on the bleachers, someone even blew an airhorn. He could only guess how many cell phones were videoing them right now.

When he'd pitched the idea to the team's head of PR, they'd loved it. Apparently, the rookie who'd come home to Texas could do no wrong.

He could only hope.

"Claire..." He exhaled shakily. Cleared his throat to start over. He was more nervous than he'd been at his first big league game. "I still remember the first time I saw you. I knew you were an all-star and I was a little leaguer."

The crowd cheered again.

"Somehow, fate decided to give me a shot with you, and I fell hard. I've never stopped falling. Every day, I find something new to love about you."

There was an audible *aww* from the crowd this time.

Claire blinked. Her eyes looked suspiciously damp, and he found himself fighting a knot in his throat.

"I want to wake up with you every day. Go to sleep with you beside me. Have some kids I can coach in little league. Whatever comes, I just want to be with you."

She squeezed his hands, hard.

"Claire, I love you. Will you marry me?"

"Yes."

Jubilation exploded in his chest. He jumped up and swept her into his arms, and off her feet. He spun them both in a circle.

The crowd was going wild. The airhorn went off again. Tons of cell phones flashed as people took pictures.

He slowed the spin to a stop and gently set her feet back on the ground.

"I love you, too," she said.

With those words, his nervousness went away. He let go of her and worked at wiggling off the diamond ring he'd jammed onto his pinkie—no pockets in his uniform.

She gasped when he placed it on her ring finger. The one carat solitaire he'd chosen glittered in the stadium lights. She could choose something different later, if she wanted. All he cared was that she'd wear his ring. That she'd said yes.

The crowd was chanting now. "Kiss! Kiss!"

When Jax looked up, he found the display on the Jumbotron had changed to the KissCam.

He grinned at his fiancée. "Guess we should give them what they want." Not that he needed an excuse.

He curved one hand behind her head, the other at her waist, and pulled her closer.

Her arms twined around his neck, and she met his kiss with a fierce gladness that tightened the ball of emotion in the back of his throat.

She was his.

And she would be forever.

She broke the kiss, blushing rosily. "You've got a game to win."

The crowd was still cheering as they came off the field hand-in-hand. He sent her through the dugout and tunnels beneath the stadium. The PR team had urged him to have her stick with a bodyguard until after the game, due to the fanfare. He was more than happy to take that advice.

The Coyotes did win the game, but that wasn't what had Jax flying high as he hurried through the after-game interviews, ready to get back to Claire.

He'd won big. He'd won Claire's heart. Not once, but twice.

EXCLUSIVE INVITATION

Are you a member of Lacy's or Susan's email newsletter? Right now you can receive a special gift, available only to newsletters subscribers. SOMEONE BLUE is a 50-page novelette and will not be released on any retailer platform—only to newsletter subscribers.

What happened to Nicholas? Will he ever find his own happily-ever-after?

Visit www.lacywilliams.net/blue and get your free gift. Unsubscribe at any time.

ALSO BY LACY WILLIAMS

SNOWBOUND IN SAWYER CREEK SERIES
(CONTEMPORARY ROMANCE)

Soldier Under the Mistletoe

The Nanny's Christmas Wish

The Rancher's Unexpected Gift

WILD WYOMING HEART SERIES (HISTORICAL
ROMANCE)

Marrying Miss Marshal

Counterfeit Cowboy

Cowboy Pride

Courted by a Cowboy

TRIPLE H BRIDES SERIES (CONTEMPORARY
ROMANCE)

Kissing Kelsey

Courting Carrie

Stealing Sarah

Keeping Kayla

Melting Megan

COWBOY FAIRYTALES SERIES (CONTEMPORARY ROMANCE)

Once Upon a Cowboy

Cowboy Charming

The Toad Prince

The Beastly Princess

The Lost Princess

HEART OF OKLAHOMA SERIES (CONTEMPORARY ROMANCE)

Kissed by a Cowboy

Love Letters from Cowboy

Mistletoe Cowboy

Cowgirl for Keeps

Jingle Bell Cowgirl

Heart of a Cowgirl

3 Days with a Cowboy

Prodigal Cowgirl

89713375R00076

Made in the USA
San Bernardino, CA
30 September 2018